Red Fire

Red Fire

Red Fire
A Quest for Awakening
BY PAULA D'ARCY

Innisfree
Press, Inc.

Published by Innisfree Press, Inc.
136 Roumfort Road
Philadelphia, PA 19119
Visit our website at www.InnisfreePress.com.

Cover art by Jean Beolan Gascoigne
"The Fold," 16 Sheepwalk Road, Stoneyford,
Lisburn, Northern Ireland BT28 3RB
(Jean_beolangascoigne@hotmail.com)

Cover design by Hugh Duffy, PhD Design
Carneys Point, New Jersey
(856-299-3316, hugh@phddesign.com)

Library of Congress Cataloging-in-Publication Data
D'Arcy, Paula (date).
Red fire: a quest for awakening / by Paula D'Arcy.
    p. cm.
ISBN 1-880913-51-8
1. Young women—Fiction. I. Title.
PS3604.A73 R4 2001
813'.54—dc21   2001024677

For Juan,
and especially for my friend Lona Damron,
who refused to let me rest
until I promised to take the original tale
called "The Stranger," written on retreat,
and allowed it to grow into this story.

Contents

ACKNOWLEDGMENTS

This manuscript has passed through many loving sets of hands! I have great esteem and gratitude for my editor, Ruth Butler, and my publisher, Marcia Broucek. They have been pure delight to work with.

As I created this story, my friend Kaye Bernard took over the arranging and booking of my speaking engagements for two years. There is no way to describe the burden she lifted from me, nor the encouragement she has given.

The gift of Jo Betsy Szebehely's home in Maine as a writing retreat was extraordinary. My heart overflows with thanks.

John Godbey has once again given up an afternoon to help me with publicity pictures. Supported by his wife, Sandra Locke Godbey, and ably assisted by my dear friends Eric and Susan Goldby, we somehow got the task done.

And to these friends who read this manuscript in varying stages of rewrites, some of them very rough, and gave such helpful guidance, I express my gratitude: Liz Halpern, Beverly Pettine (my sister), Ric Cox, Sharon Anderson, Terry Rush, Mike Leach, Kathleen Niendorff, Howard Hovde, Chuck Huffman, Millie Migues, Macrina Wiederkehr, Tammy Greer, Susan Goldby, Keith and Andrea Miller.

There is a plane of existence that to us is very real.
Within this reality we raise our families, publish newspapers,
shop for food and clothing, marvel at the world's artistry,
form governments, and create laws for the common good.
Moving inside of these agreements,
we work together with purpose and possibility,
never questioning the appearance of things.
Yet within this experience, even as we live it,
there is something else which knows us,
and which is calling us to itself.
In the midst of full and complicated lives, it is there.
But while many things in life clamor for our attention,
this Presence will not force itself to be heard
above the competing sounds of our coveted routines.
It waits, shimmering, at the edges of our imagination.
Only the opening of the heart calls it forward,
and only the spirit within is able to know it.
Everything else is an echo.
As we experience the moments we call our "lifetime,"
there is always the dilemma between
choosing to see only the lesser plane of existence,
or to awaken.

INTRODUCTION

In September of 1997, a wonderfully generous friend in Austin, Texas, Jo Betsy Szebehely, offered my friend Macrina Wiederkehr her home on the Maine coast for a writing retreat. Macrina gratefully accepted and invited another writer, Joyce Rupp, and me to join her. Our days there had their own rhythm. We each arose and worked silently through the day in our separate niches, both inside and outside the house. At dinner we broke the mood of quiet and work to create wonderful meals and share the struggles of our writing. Usually we built a fire. Often we walked outside to savor the stars, or read snatches of our writings, new and old, for feedback and encouragement.

At night I pitched a small tent on the deck, overlooking the bluff and the sea. Sleeping there night after night eased me into nature's rhythm. I was reading a fantasy tale, *The Last Unicorn*, a favorite of Macrina's from childhood. I felt like a child in the tent at night, many evenings listening to rain splash onto the stretch of nylon that covered my little world. Some nights I actually felt the water as it pushed its way through the seams of my enclosure. Then I'd edge closer to the dry corners of the tent, my flashlight still focused on the pages of my reading. I slept deep and well, listening to the voice of the rain.

I came to Maine with bagloads of journals, prepared to write in the diary style of my first four books. I had a sense of the material I wanted to use. But in the first morning, a story spoke to me that I had not expected to tell. It is my own experience, yet clearly not mine alone. It is about the journey toward awakening, a passage that comes to each person in distinct and beautiful ways.

I let the story tell itself to me during those warm and foggy September days. In the telling, rather than writing in the first person, I become a young girl named Anastasia, and the story of my inner journey assumes an outer form. The experience is described within a tale which includes a small town, a forest, a Stranger and a visitor named Tenar. Certainly Tenar taught me that Love is a power so brilliant we shade our eyes in its shadow.

I hope this story will give you a taste of the wonder that emerges when you find yourself disturbed by an inner beckoning and decide to pursue it. As fantasy, there is no attempt made to resolve how people ate, or found shelter or endured the elements. It is not an adventure story where the heroine returns in the end with enough beans to feed the town. Nor is this an attempt to describe God as you may already understand God in your own faith tradition. If you read searching for familiar images, you will be disappointed.

I hope you *will* encounter what your heart has not yet seen. The opening of the heart is not part of the fantasy. That is the part that's true. I invite you to go to the edge of the forest with Anastasia and decide what it is you really want. Will you risk experiencing what no one prepared you to foresee?

If you cannot read this story in a tent in the rain, at least try to read it as a child. And perhaps, from somewhere deep within, you will hear the call of awakening, feel the Red Fire that burns in the secret chambers of your heart.

Imagine yourself standing atop a bluff. In every direction are mountain ranges of great grandeur. Your eyes have always focused on just one or two of those distant peaks. But suddenly you sense that all around you may be glory. You climb onto a great, flat rock at the bluff's edge and slowly begin to turn around.

As you move, you are aware of a growing stillness. You sense that all the things your eyes are taking in have *always* been there, and have always spoken of the greatest things. You search the landscape and know that everything is familiar. But truly, although you've looked, you never saw it before. In that moment a Knowing stirs within you, and your soul begins to awaken.

Red Fire

"Power can force obedience.

Only love can summon a response of love."

—*Philip Yancey*

Part One
The Stranger

Long ago two small towns nestled along the banks of a great river. One Town was named Status, the other, Quo. This is where Anastasia was born. And since the population of each town was less than a hundred people, years ago the towns decided to govern their affairs jointly. There was one Town Manager, one School Board, one Committee for Zoning and Planning. And the primary purpose of each was to make sure that Nothing Ever Changed.

Town Meetings were held on Tuesday evenings at seven-thirty PM, whether or not there was business to conduct. But generally there was business, for it is more difficult than might be imagined to stem the tide of change. It takes great vigilance and energy. The Town Manager often lamented that if it were not for towns-people periodically trying to introduce new ideas, life would be perfect and easily managed.

The Town Manager of Status and Quo was a clever man. He was large and round, his great belly preceding him as he walked with a heavy step down the town's cobbled streets. His hair had long since fallen away, as if it had flown from the sound of his loud voice, so filled with Authority. His complexion was ruddy, his sideburns bristly and black, and he had impatient fingers that continually touched and twirled the stray hairs of his wiry moustache.

The Town Manager knew everyone, and everyone knew him. He liked it that way. It meant many perks in the businesses around town. It meant influence. Power. How else could the mindless repetition of endless conversations and actions be ensured if the Town Manager did not have this control? All rules and regulations were written down in a large black book called the Book of Laws, which he kept safely stored in a weathered leather chest beneath his desk.

The good people of Status and Quo believed there was a God who watched over their villages. God could not be seen, but certain men in the towns were thought to hold special knowledge of what appeased this God, and what God was truly like. These men were greatly respected and recognized by the townspeople as the All-Knowing Ones. Their ideas about the ways of God were the Authority, and they alone decided which beliefs about God were correct. Their views were informed by studying the life of a man named Jesus, who lived and walked on the earth two-thousand years before.

The All-Knowing Ones attested to the fact that "He lives," even today. But, in reality, they taught that nothing was valid unless it looked like the past. It was not thought that a person might freshly meet the one who "lives" if that experience did not agree with the parameters of God that were already clearly drawn and meticulously guarded. Their teachings leaned toward safer things, like Scholarship, Being Right, and Memorizing the permissible knowledge.

Consequently, bubbling young children were frequently drilled on events in the lives of religious ancestors and the nature of "acceptable" experiences. The children were proud of the facts they memorized and could recite many things.

Thus things in Status and Quo ran very smoothly. The shops hummed and all ceremonies for the worship of God were appropriately formal and well-organized. The past was revered and the future seemed to be secure. Life in Status and Quo went along in its protective rhythm of work, produce, stay the same. WORK, PRODUCE, STAY THE SAME.

Until the Stranger arrived, and it all began to change.

He dropped into Status in a gleaming silver machine that had great wings, like an eagle. No one had ever seen anything like it. He claimed to have come from the Great Mountains, far to the east. Legend held that within those Mountains was the river's Secret Source. The Town Manager felt that such tales only produced questions, and longings. So it was forbidden to talk about the Mountains or the river.

But here, on this day, was a Stranger announcing that he had seen those Mountains. Indeed, that he lived there. And he said it all with great delight. He called his machine "Silver Bird," and said he used it to enjoy Beauty and ride the Wind. He had been doing just that when he discovered Status and Quo.

Everything about the Stranger was a contradiction. Pinned above his shirt pocket was a pair of wings that meant he had been well-trained on his silver machine.

Yet when he ran his fingers through his thick hair, he seemed young and boyish. His taut and powerful muscles hinted at a hidden strength, but in his eyes was a mischievous, merry twinkle. He was such a mystery of unpredictability that it flustered the Town Manager, who could not decide how to react to him or what to do.

The Stranger's pockets were memorable, all filled with trinkets and surprises. Small trees to plant. Keys. Sugar delights. Newborn kittens. Tickets to carnivals. He jingled as he walked. Suddenly, in mid-step, he would reach into a pocket and perhaps pull out a nut, tossing it to a grateful squirrel. "Oh, let's see what I have in the depths of these vast pockets," he would laugh, reaching down and shaking things up inside. Then he would laugh again. He was a person with no sense of solemnity. Only joy.

On the day he arrived, the Stranger marched into the

center of town and rented a small room above the bakery. "He seems inclined to stay for a little while," the old women whispered. Wherever he went, their eyes followed him.

When the Stranger encountered townspeople, he was polite but always told the truth. If someone mumbled, "How are you?" he considered it a true request and stopped to tell them. It made the adults uncomfortable but amused the children.

As it happened, the Stranger settled into a pleasant life in the towns of Status and Quo. He laughed heartily, spoke cheerfully, and was an endless source of fun and play. The children met him in the playground after school, where he made every game the greatest pleasure.

One summer morning the Stranger waited to meet the children as they were leaving their classes for Training and Memorization. The children followed him to a nearby park, and once there he motioned for them to sit around him in a circle. The Stranger suddenly looked at little Anastasia and asked her to tell him what she knew in her heart about God.

Anastasia was the youngest and smallest child in her family. She had fiery black eyes, and soft dark ringlets framed her face. Even as she scrambled after her brothers, scaling fences and climbing trees, there was a lightness and gentleness about her. It softened the earnestness that often caused her brow to furrow and her nose to wrinkle. At times Anastasia seemed far away in reverie until someone called her name. Then she would startle and remember to rejoin the games.

As she tried to think of what to say to the Stranger, Anastasia's dark eyes grew wide. Finally, her chin quivered. She would have done anything for him, and she wanted to answer correctly. But no one had told her what this answer was. She knew only how to memorize and repeat.

Long moments passed, and tears began to form in Anastasia's shining eyes. She looked at the ground and fingered the rag doll she was carrying. Seeing her distress, the Stranger lifted her up and placed her gently on his knee. A pussy willow mysteriously appeared from his top shirt pocket, and Anastasia smiled in spite of her tears. He looked lovingly at all the children for a long while. Several got up from where they had been sitting and moved even closer, stretching out next to the Stranger on the grass. He never asked them to be still, but he was so still himself that, one by one, they became very quiet.

With quick hands the Stranger reached out and began collecting the lists of facts and events the children had copied for their lessons. As they watched, he folded their papers in unusual and intriguing ways. They were fascinated. Adding string and ribbon from his pockets, he kept shaping the paper until dozens of colorful shapes had been created. The Stranger kept working. Each time he completed a new shape, he tied it cleverly to the last one until there was a long series of colored papers attached to a single string with bright ribbons.

"A kite!" cried one of the younger boys.

When the kite was finished, the Stranger stopped and looked for the longest while into the heavens, as if he were speaking silently to the sky. No one moved. At first, the children felt only the smallest puff of air, a gentle breeze. They waited. Another puff appeared, followed by the next push of air. The papers and ribbons fluttered for a moment. Then great gusts of air began to stir until, finally, right where the children stood, a warm, strong wind arose. It lifted the new kite over their heads, and soon it was riding above the trees. The children tipped back their heads to watch, and as they did, the Stranger told them this story:

"Long ago," he said, "in a Kingdom where there is no sadness and no time, there was a Beautiful Being who was bright and glowing and knew all things. This Being was pure delight. But one thing could add to this Being's joy: if the Being could have a shape, a form—truly, many forms—that could express love. So a great idea was born: The Being would create human life!

"This would unfold slowly and carefully," the Stranger continued, "and wherever life existed, the Being would live deep within it, disguised and hidden, directing, guiding, and loving the creation. Filling life with the Being's own delight."

The Stranger paused to look at the children thoughtfully,

choosing each word with care. "An idea is always just the beginning. For it to become real, the Being needed a great stage. A time and place for life to appear. A place where things could live and be. The great stage would be called Earth.

"But the Being did not create Earth quickly. Earth became slowly. The particles of life to which the Great Being gave birth began to take shape and grow. Everything the Being created contained the Being's Light. The Being's Spirit. The same Essence. The same Heart."

The Stranger paused and reached into the outside pocket of his jacket, producing a small, red glove. With great effort he worked to fit his large hand and long fingers into that small glove. It took a while. The children began to think about what it was like for something large to make itself become very small. As they followed the Stranger's story, they imagined a Being, filled with love, fitting its Spirit into stones, trees, and spider webs. Creating the water in the river. Placing the fire of its Presence within all life. This was magic. Real magic.

The Stranger continued his telling. "Very slowly the small pieces created by the great Being joined and became air and light. Water, earth, and fire. And the Soul of the Being began to shine in the heavens each day in what we call the sun, giving warmth and life to every form. Think about that. Imagine what it would take to make something so wondrous, which burns so brightly . . . a sun that is far away in the heavens, yet burns across millions and millions of miles." As he spoke, the sun beat down on their faces, warming them, shining through the trees, coaxing the leaves to grow.

"Eventually the pieces of life multiplied into stars, rivers, streams, and waterfalls. Oceans. Seed-bearing plants.

Trees of every shape and description. You know that an acorn, small enough to fit into a baby's palm, gives birth to an oak tree a hundred feet high. Only the Being could create this. No one else. The Being could fashion birds and enter atoms. The Being could give birth to the moon and teach it to live in harmony with the waters. Still the Being went on creating. Seasons. Every species of sea life. Fish. Reptiles. Insects. All mammals. The varieties of winged ones, from the hummingbird to the eagle."

The Stranger paused. "Can you picture it? The Being created a garden, providing food for each species and each kind. Fruit trees. Berries. Roots. Flowers. Grains. Grasses." He picked up a handful of grass and sprinkled it into the air. The children giggled as it fell on their heads and arms. They touched it, wondering about the Being who had created this, fitting its own greatness inside.

"Over and over again," the Stranger went on, "with millenniums passing, this great Being continued to burst forth in blazing expressions of Beauty. The lives and cycles of these forms is called Nature. To Her was given the right to reign in this new kingdom. Within Her lie the secrets of the beginning. She watched then, and watches now, as it still unfolds. And She will tell you Her secrets if you are quiet, and listen. But if you ignore Her, or treat Her carelessly, She will hide from you. And that is a very great loss indeed, because when you can see Her, you can know the Being and the Power that called all those particles together to create this great stage for Love."

"What about the people?" asked Anastasia, her eyes watching the Stranger intensely as he told his story.

The Stranger smiled. "Yes, finally it was time for you to appear!" He leaned forward and pushed Anastasia's nose with his thumb, making a squeaking sound. Everyone smiled. Then the Stranger's eyes filled with tenderness. "This glowing Being now unfolded the form of a Human Being. And the Great Being called the Human Being a living image."

The children grew still. It is doubtful that they understood those words. But they knew the Stranger was saying something important. They felt it.

"The design of the Human Being was the most difficult. Everything else that had been created was simple in this way: a flower was content to be a flower. A fish, a fish. A tree, a tree. But to each Human Being was given a mind." He tapped his head. "A creative mind capable of thinking about things. A mind that can see things clearly, but doesn't always do so. A mind that can make mistakes, sometimes believing things that are not true at all. A mind that is even capable of forgetting that the

Human Being is created in the Great Being's image. A mind that can think there is no Beautiful Being causing everything to be.

"To the Human Being was also given a sense of being unique. Everyone experiences him- or herself as 'me.' An individual. No two of you are exactly alike. But at the same time that you are uniquely you, you are also much more. Each of you is one of the Being's wonderful disguises. On the inside, everyone is really the same . . . everyone is an expression of the Beautiful Being."

The children looked around at each other for several minutes. Smiles appeared on some faces. Some embarrassed giggles broke out. It was funny, somehow, to look at someone else and consider that you weren't different, deep inside. Only the way you looked was different. Only the outside.

The children had been sitting for a long while, and almost at the same moment everyone stood up to stretch their arms and legs. Even the kite stretched, moving out over the river. Many took off their socks and shoes and waded in the water. The Stranger watched them play. When they tired of their games, they pulled the kite down and placed it carefully on the grass. The children again circled the Stranger, and one of the older girls asked, "It is magic, isn't it?"

"It is magic," he said softly. "On the dry land, on the bottom of the waters, life is growing. It is alive, still becoming. And the Beautiful Being is hidden inside each part of life. Every seed has the power to grow, new life after new life. Creation will always continue if we care for it with love.

"And you . . . " He looked at the children for a long while, for he saw the fire that was deep within them, "you were made with great care. And lest you ever lose your way, the Being placed inside of you a Knowing. When you listen for that Knowing, you will recognize the Being's Spirit in you. It will remind you who you truly are. You will remember you cannot be separated from the Being who gave you life, and you do not have to be afraid."

As the Stranger finished his story, he motioned for the children to follow him. They joined hands, making a great circle, and danced and laughed and sang into the Wind, their skirts and shirt tails blowing. When the children left for home, each one carried in his or her hand a piece of the magic. A leaf. A cluster of pine needles. A piece of moss. A sparkling stone. An acorn. A flower. Anastasia's own small hand held a fistful of soil.

Of course the kite was seen by the adults. When it was later found to have been made out of the children's lessons, many of the adults were very displeased. Then it was learned that the children had all been dancing. Dancing! Dancing while mothers called them for dinner. Dancing when they might have been studying the Book of Laws, or reading about the past. Dancing while there were chores waiting to be done. Dancing on Sunday! What would happen if everyone danced?

But the children now knew that creation itself danced. Wasn't the moon spinning in a circle around the land and sea? Wasn't the land and sea a ball that was spinning, too? Weren't the heavens sprinkled with stars, and everything filled with the Great Being, through and through. Wasn't that God? Wasn't the light of the sun God's light? If that were true, then no matter where you were, God would be touching you. Maybe the God who lived beyond the Mountains was not hidden at all. It seemed amazing and wonderful. The words and thoughts of the children bubbled and gleamed in the air.

But the adults of Status and Quo feared their merriment, and the town elders fussed and fumed and worked themselves into a very unhappy state.

One prominent member of the All-Knowing Ones could only stammer, "But of course God loves the way things are! Why would God want to change anything?" Even as he spoke, clouds swept overhead, moving into shapes and sizes of incredible variety, lasting only for seconds until they became the next form. The eldest member steamed, "How dare this Stranger teach the children that they can recognize God on their own? They need us to tell them what is true!" He thought of all the knowledge he alone possessed.

Status and Quo were in an uproar. Then mysterious things began to happen. In their classrooms the children began to question what they were told and had always accepted. "If we all came from the Beautiful Being, why do the elders think some people are better than others? If the Great Being gives life to all things, why don't we speak of this all the time, not just for an hour on Sunday? If the Great Being filled us with delight, why don't we dance more often?"

The Town Manager formed committees and held meetings to deal with the chaos. There were no grounds to arrest the Stranger, for he had committed no crime. So one All-Knowing One was selected to visit him and suggest, with great tact, that given the present state of things, he might be happier somewhere else.

The Stranger replied that he was equally happy wherever he was.

Committees met again. They argued and agonized. At last, in desperation, the Town Manager, consulting the Book of Laws, decided to take matters into his own hands. By evening, two days later, the Stranger could no longer find a room to rent in Status or Quo, nor a diner to serve him a meal. Understanding, he gathered his few possessions and got ready to leave. He could have slipped noiselessly out of town, preparing the Silver Bird quietly and stealing into the darkness. But he truly loved, and love has its own demands.

So that night, before going, he gathered the children in the park to say good-bye. Several of them cried and begged him to stay. Their lives had been different while he was with them, and they did not want to return to a life of routine and sameness. But the action of the Town Manager had set many things in motion.

And so, after looking once more into the children's faces, the Stranger stepped into the silver flying machine. Anastasia stood quietly watching as it lifted above the tree tops and entered a cloud, finally disappearing into the softness. After a while even the sound of the wings against the wind could not be heard. The only noises were the sounds of night coming to Status and Quo.

The adults of the towns of Status and Quo breathed a collective sigh of relief and went back to business as usual. WORK, PRODUCE, STAY THE SAME. WORK, PRODUCE, STAY THE SAME. Board meetings continued to be held at seven-thirty PM on Tuesday evenings, whether or not there was business to conduct. Classrooms returned to teaching the children to memorize facts. Proposed changes were sent to committees, where they were safely delayed.

And nothing appeared to have changed at all.

Red Fire

"One does not discover new lands without consenting

to lose sight of the shore for a very long time."

—*Andre Gide*

Part Two
The Magician

Paula D'Arcy

Childhood is an unparalleled time. If one is fortunate, it is a time of romping and laughter, of games and delight. Of course, many are not so blessed. For them, childhood is a time of terror and fear. But for most persons, regardless of fortune, a curious phenomenon still occurs: in time, the everyday details of childhood are largely forgotten. The specifics of events, large and small, grow dim. Isolated moments will stand out, but thousands of smaller ones grow weak. Most adults could not describe an ordinary day when they were six, or when they were four.

So it was for Anastasia. For many nights after the Stranger left town, she held her handful of soil, collected in a white lace hanky, and cried herself to sleep. She watched the sky, always believing he would return. At first, when she and the other children were alone, they talked endlessly about the Stranger and his words, about how he had made them feel. But soon Anastasia began to wonder if she had not made some of it up. Then one night her little hanky of soil spilled onto the floor beside her bed. The hanky got washed. Soon her memories began to seem like a dream.

Months went by and she watched the sky less often. Eventually, she stopped looking to the clouds and got busily caught up with her friends and new lessons in school. There were also many household chores that filled up her days, such as helping her father plant a garden or baking with her mother.

The years came and went without any major struggles, yet as Anastasia grew older she began to feel increasingly unhappy. There seemed to be no particular reason for her discontent. Her family was kind enough. She was an obedient student in school, and soon her studies would be completed. Sometimes she and her brothers took long hikes along the river, or challenged one another to fifty-yard races. In those moments her cheeks were flushed, and laughter filled all their hearts. But the melancholy inevitably returned. Anastasia kept feeling there must be something more.

And then something happened. Tentatively, at first, and then with growing fascination, Anastasia began to develop a friendship with a young man in Status named Peter. Her heart sang when he appeared at her door, sometimes with a bouquet of hand-picked flowers, or with clumsily wrapped treasures from the river bed. The adults in Status and Quo smiled and exchanged glances when the two young lovers passed by. Peter was tall and lanky, and Anastasia often seemed to be swallowed up by his long cloak as they walked along together. The happiness they found in each other's company lit the corners where they passed. Peter wrote a poem for Anastasia which included the lines,

"One alone would be buffeted by the wind,
but together we are like a strong tree, able to bear any storm."

Anastasia found herself writing in little notebooks that she hid underneath her mattress, tucking the pages far into the bedding. She wrote whimsical poems and poured out her feelings on the pages. Sometimes she drew pictures or sketched flowers along the margins. It became a struggle to keep up with her lessons when other things attracted her so much more. In the library she found books that spoke to her heart, and she shared these stories with Peter. For them, the plain world of Status and Quo was filled with color and delight.

In her classes on religion, Anastasia grew impatient, and her questions were considered impertinent by the teachers. "If God created us in love," she wanted to know, "then why are you teaching us to be afraid? How can you be certain that there isn't much more to know about

God than we already believe?" These questions tried the patience of her teachers, who only wanted Anastasia to accept what they told her.

This caused Anastasia a great deal of distress. She was filled with questions, but she still wanted to satisfy her teachers and obey all the rules. It seemed as if love were causing her to see everything differently.

As soon as Anastasia finished her studies, Peter gave her a ring of intention. But in the midst of joyous preparations for their wedding, a wagon piled with bricks that Peter was unloading lost its wheel and collapsed, killing him instantly. To Anastasia, the loss felt like her own death. She was surrounded by the family and friends who had always loved her, but they watched with concern as her complexion grew pale, and life seemed to leave her eyes.

Dark months followed.

Anastasia grew increasingly silent. She no longer asked her continuous questions. No answer would bring Peter back, and with him her hope had disappeared. It grew more difficult for her to wrestle with the sorrow within and still try to meet everyone's expectations. In her journal she wrote:

Everyone is so anxious for me to get better. They don't want me to hurt. But I do hurt . . . every cell and every bone. How I long to be "me" again, but I don't know how to find that person. I no longer know who I am.

I wonder where Peter is now? Does he miss me? Will I catch up with him one day, or will I always be left behind?

And how do I grieve what I didn't have? How do I grieve for a dream?

In time, Anastasia began to work in the town of Quo, assisting in the library. For the next few years she cataloged and stacked books. One day as she searched for a reference book that had been misplaced, she opened a small closet and found two old boxes that had been pushed far beneath a shelf. She opened the first box and read the titles aloud. The box contained books about Philosophy. Psychology. Art. Her mind raced. One by one she brought the books home and read late into the night. Each subject fed a growing hunger. Not only did the books expand her world, they also brought new understanding to her heart. Her mind searched everything for meaning. She paused for a long while when she read,

"The greatest enemy of what you need to learn
is what you believe you already know."

In the library the presence of the children gave her moments of joy. But it did not remove her restlessness or the sudden waves of sadness. It was a great strain to understand what the love she had tasted had to do with the ordinary life now surrounding her. It was particularly difficult because that very life appeared to bring contentment to everyone else. No matter how deeply she wished the world of Status and Quo could satisfy her, as it once had, it no longer did.

Then one day, while planting flowers for her mother, Anastasia's hand stopped as she kneeled to turn over a spadeful of soil. She looked at the soil for the longest while, touching it gently with her finger. The soil wasn't dead. That much was clear. It responded to her touch and in some strange way was communicating to her. She gathered up a small handful of earth and sat back on her heels. As she listened deep within, everything around her became still. She felt a stir of connection with the bit of soil she held in her hand, and her loneliness lessened. And in that moment she knew *something* was calling her.

That very afternoon Anastasia started to pack a few belongings into a knapsack. Each day, while she continued to go about her daily routine, she added an item or two, telling no one of her plans. But the hours of each day were no longer ordinary. The Knowing she'd felt as she held the soil continued to press from within. Late one evening she wrote in her notebook:

How strongly I am suddenly drawn to cross the river and climb those Mountains that stretch far to the east. Some-where, within those hills, the Stranger lives. I know it. I feel it. His words from long ago keep filling my heart and call to me. This is the first thing to make sense in a long, long while. The soil reminded me. Somehow I know that if I find him, I will find me.

Before the next waning of the moon, on a clear, starry night, Anastasia gathered her few belongings and slipped away from the only home she had ever known. She was leaving everything she had always thought her life would be. Every treasured dream. Her heart ached, yet she did not turn back. She walked steadily into the night.

By morning, Anastasia had arrived at a secret place she knew, where the river met the hills near the foot of the Mountains. Crouched against a marbled outcropping of rock, her small body shivering against the cold stone, she watched as first light announced itself in rolling waves of lavender. Streaks of clouds formed layers between the bursts of light, creating patterns. Her eyes followed the moving mosaic. Second by second, the sky changed, each new arrangement of dawn filling the heavens, each color deeper than the one before.

Caught in that splendor, she sat motionless, barely drawing a breath. How many such mornings had the earth witnessed since the beginning of time, each as gloriously and uniquely beautiful?

She continued to watch. The light of dawn appeared so distinct from the darkness of the night. Yet she remembered the Stranger teaching the children that even though things might look different on the outside, deep within, nothing was different at all. Everything was an expression of the Great Being's spirit. The Stranger had said so many things that she wondered about now. She needed to know more.

As Anastasia watched, flocks of geese rose up from the east and flew in great, long lines over the water. It seemed as if Dawn were chasing them, sending them to catch the awakening day.

The first months of the journey were unusually difficult. Many times Anastasia wanted to turn back to the safety of her familiar life. She even wondered if she were thinking clearly.

'This is not me,' she would muse. 'This is not the me I know . . . or any me I've ever been. I feel like I'm living in a dream.' At night she gathered pine boughs and laid them in a soft pile in the shelter of the tallest trees. Wrapping a worn grey blanket around her shoulders, she lay on the bed of earth and watched the stars.

It was confusing to have finally followed what seemed to call her so strongly, and yet feel so alone and afraid. She wondered why the Stranger didn't appear. She began to doubt herself. The Stranger had taught that even though Human Beings were capable of seeing clearly, it was also possible to make a mistake. Was she mistaken about him?

She ate berries and shared nuts with the squirrels. Clouds and trees became her companions. Birds taught her how to dip into the river for fish. Each dawn she waited for the comfort of the sun. But as the days passed, her despair gained force. She had already climbed far into the Mountains, and there was still no trace of the one for whom she searched.

"Nothing is happening," she mourned. "Nothing."

She remembered many of the Stranger's stories, but recalling his words no longer seemed to hold the power they once had. It was only this strange summons from deep within herself that gave her the will to go on.

Many cycles of the moon passed, and Anastasia found herself spending more and more time in a growing circle of quiet. She walked for hours, following the sound of the waterfalls. Something out there knew her. It pursued her and beckoned her, both.

One night she pulled out her worn notebook and wrote:

*If I knew nothing . . . if I had been taught nothing . . .
still, the Great Being would know me. And would walk
with me all my days, waiting for my heart to awaken.
And whether or not I was aware of it, that same God who
loved into being the petal of the smallest flower, the gla-
cier, the deer, the rock, the galaxies of stars, would know
the deepest part of me.*

Anastasia closed her notebook and lay her head beside it.
The words had poured from her heart. She did not recognize how similar they were to thoughts the Stranger had
spoken to the children in Status and Quo. The difference
was that it had been *his* telling, then. Now the Knowing,
somehow, was hers.

As she walked, Anastasia often remembered Peter, her
family, and friends, and she thought of time passing in
Status and Quo. If she had stayed, she would still be reading many books, acquiring more and more instruction.

What had she gained by leaving? Her only companions now were the plants and animals. The Mountains.

The trees had become her teachers. Sometimes she would sit for long hours, until her breathing matched the breathing of the branches. She was learning to pay careful attention to everything. To the birds in flight. The color of the grains. The tiniest pebble.

Sometimes, if she found a pasture, she would put her cheek against the warm grass and listen to the beating of the earth's heart. And if she listened through the stillness and calm that were growing within her, she could feel Nature's rhythms and recognize the earth's heartbeat within herself.

She now understood what the Stranger had meant when he said, "She will tell you her secrets if you are quiet and listen."

Some days she found it impossible to keep her spirits high, and she wrestled with questions about the mystery of things. Some days she felt foolish to be so preoccupied with her pursuit of the Stranger. Still, the longing was there. The Stranger was the reason she had begun this journey. What if she never found him . . . never succeeded?

With her doubts came greater fear. 'Perhaps I should have stayed in Status and Quo,' she thought, 'and accepted the answers given to me. Not questioned things, or begun this quest.' Everything churned within. Should she go back? Go forward? Where *was* forward? And was going back even possible?

That summer Anastasia camped in a grove of pine trees that formed a semicircle on the peak of a beautiful mountain bluff. Now, Fall approached. On a particular morning she arose early and took a leisurely walk to greet the animals and visit some remaining clusters of wildflowers. She picked a small bouquet of Queen Anne's lace and walked thoughtfully back into the shelter of pines. Warmed by the sun, she sat gazing at the valley below.

So lost was Anastasia in her reverie that she did not hear or see a dark figure approaching. The unexpected visitor was almost at her shoulder when she startled and looked up. Though her heart beat fiercely, her voice remained strangely calm.

"Who are you?" she finally managed to say. She had not seen another human being for a very long time.

"Who are *you*?" the newcomer asked. Appearing overdressed for walking in the forest, the visitor wore a long, dark wrap and a black felt hat with silver buttons decorating the band.

"But I asked first," she countered.

The figure smiled, watching her carefully. "Yes, you did."

Anastasia waited. Her visitor kept looking at her with a strong gaze, and kindly, knowing eyes. At least, that is what she felt, that this person knew many things. Where did that feeling come from?

The figure continued to watch Anastasia, almost seeming to read her thoughts, or to have a different way of seeing her. Everything about this person was compelling, unlike anyone she had ever known.

Finally, the visitor smiled again. "I cannot tell you my true name, but you may call me Tenar."

"Tenar." She repeated it slowly. "Tenar. It is not a name I have ever heard. But it does suit you."

"And you, do *you* have a name?"

"Oh, yes, I'm sorry. I am Anastasia."

"Anastasia." Tenar said it quietly. "And what is one named Anastasia doing in these Mountains?"

With a rush of emotion Anastasia found herself telling Tenar the story of her love, and then her heartache. She spoke of her long search for the Stranger, whom she had met as a child. She told of his flying machine, his stories, and his ideas, that haunted her still. Even as she talked, she could not imagine why she was trusting someone she did not know with such private feelings, but she let herself speak from her heart.

Then she added, "Do you know the Stranger? Have you heard of him? Can you help me find him? Do you know the way?"

Tenar stood still, looking into Anastasia's dark eyes, watching her but not speaking. Several moments passed. Finally she heard the words, "Yes, Anastasia, I could lead you to the Stranger. But to fulfill such a great request, I would need something in return."

"Oh, anything. Anything!" Anastasia cried.

Tenar smiled and took her hands. "Anastasia, you should not speak words you are not prepared to mean."

"But I *do* mean them," she protested.

Tenar spoke gently. "Begin by listening to me. I will be content for you to become my assistant, of sorts. My pupil."

"Of course," Anastasia interrupted in a rush. "And it doesn't matter what you teach. I will learn. I do hope it is not math, because I am much better in English and literature. But even if it is math, I will learn." She spoke every word without taking a breath.

Laughing out loud, Tenar replied, "I do not teach reading or math, Anastasia." After a pause, her new teacher asked her, "Do you know what you truly want? It's important. Do you know what you want more than anything? Look inside before you answer, and then it will be clear to you whether or not you want to come with me. I am not a teacher, Anastasia. I am a Magician."

The single word "Magician" filled the air. This was the last thing Anastasia had expected. She could not make the idea fit comfortably inside of her. She felt unsettled and frightened. She looked at Tenar and became very still. Minutes passed, and neither Anastasia nor Tenar moved. It was as if time had stopped.

Continuing to hold her eyes, the Magician went on: "If you decide to come with me, you will begin to see things that may be hard to look at. How much do you want to see?"

Still Anastasia did not move. As she stood quietly wondering how to respond, a large pool began to appear in front of her. Fascinated, she watched as things hidden in her mind began to become visible in the magic waters. Then with increasing alarm, she saw her fears take shape and begin to walk toward her with menacing purpose. She saw her fear of not being right. Or perfect. Or important. Her fear of not being loved. Of not measuring up. Of not being good enough. Of not being special. Of not deserving. Her fear of change. Her fear of risking things, only to fail. Her fear of being alone. All the fears that had ever held her back marched by, as if on parade.

Suddenly Anastasia saw what she knew she was meant to

see: All her fears had been a means of great protection. Fear had been the reason she had accepted life in Status and Quo for so many years. Fear provided the excuse she had given herself for not challenging the elders' narrow, limited ideas. Fear was the reason she had tried so hard to please others, unwilling to risk confrontation or change.

Overwhelmed by her memories, she continued to gaze into the pool.

This time she saw her old hurts and pains begin to swirl in the water, turning the pool into a murky brew. As each pain surfaced to the top, she saw bruises that were years past. She saw hurts she had used to get others to notice her and feel sympathy. Old sufferings caused little whirling eddies that made the water even muddier. Distresses she thought she had long forgotten collected in stagnant pools.

Unexpectedly, images of people in Status and Quo came into her mind. She remembered how they lived their lives focusing on events that had happened long ago. She hadn't guessed it was also true of her. But she was seeing it now . . . watching it in the magic pool. Her clinging to things. Wanting nothing to change. Wanting to be in control, just like the elders of Status and Quo had wanted to control her. Most of all, she saw how clinging to the past left her arms and hands full. She had no freedom to reach out for the gift of each new day.

Even as Anastasia fought to understand all she was looking at, the images in the pool shifted once again. This time she saw all the cautions and hesitations that had filled her life. She saw herself standing stiff and frozen, unwilling to move. Choosing safety rather than seeking to find out what she could become. Choosing sameness rather than risking disapproval. Choosing a mask of "looking good" rather than making choices from her heart.

This new awareness caused Anastasia to shut her eyes briefly and draw a deep breath.

How often had she criticized the people in Status and Quo for their blind acceptance of the Book of Laws? But in reality, perhaps she was no different. She had never truly risked being independent. She had only appeared to be that way. When she began this journey to the Mountains, her choice had seemed brave. Now she understood that even *that* bold step had been within her control. No one had challenged any beliefs she did not want challenged. No one had touched or exposed conclusions she did not want disturbed.

But this moment was different . . . because a Magician might challenge everything: her fears, her clinging to safety, her hesitancy to be *herself*. It was happening already. Now she could see how much easier it was to dream about change than to change. 'I only wanted to find the Stranger,' she thought. 'I didn't want to change my life. How has it come to this?'

She looked around. The Mountains were now familiar. The animals. The trees. Her journey had resulted in some new thoughts, but she had not been asked to change. Now it was clear to her how comforting it had been to only *read or think* or *speak* about things . . . but not to actually *change*. In the end, she was no different from the people in Status and Quo; STAY THE SAME had been her motto, too.

Just as she was criticizing herself the most harshly for this weakness, a large, menacing creature with angry, blood-red eyes and green scales appeared in front of her in the magic pool. It laughed wickedly and seemed ready to leap up from the pool and attack her. Instinctively Anastasia stepped back. In that instant, she recognized the creature for what it truly was: the critic inside of her.

A critic who had the power to keep her from loving herself.

She cried tenderly. Her heart ached. To really change was more difficult than she had ever imagined. She had so many fears. And now she saw that she didn't even know how to truly love herself. She had loved a *dream* of herself. She had loved a *picture* of her life.

Almost as if in response to her thoughts, the pool's sparkling reflections rose in waves of color. Anastasia knew she was watching her romantic dreams and fantasies. Her wish to be cherished and taken care of. The secret corners of her heart. She even saw her longing to find the Stranger that had driven her to this place. But the pool was making it clear that even this longing was limited by her ideas of how her quest should happen.

What if it happened in a different way?

What if there was something beyond what she could see? Would she allow herself to find it? Was she willing to risk the unknown in order to find her way?

At last, Anastasia looked again into the Magician's eyes. The Magician had asked her, "What do you truly want?" Now she asked herself: Did she want to grow, or to stay the same? Was something real beckoning her, or was this quest the gravest mistake of her life? What was more foolhardy, to stay or to go?

A deeper voice said GO. It was like an inner fire, directing her from within.

There was no one to help her decide. There were no guarantees. No certainties. Only the voice speaking deep within her belly. Could she trust herself?

As Anastasia studied the Magician's eyes, they appeared

to hold many things. Love and tenderness. Power. Detachment. Passion. One moment they were unfathomable, then in the next they seemed to see inside of her, pulling her from within. Her own eyes filled with tears as she felt the Mystery and Knowing behind that gaze.

She sensed the time had come to decide. What did she want? What did she *truly* want? She trembled. And in that moment the pool slowly disappeared. Now the only thing in front of Anastasia was Tenar, waiting.

Something within her trusted this Magician, but she could not explain why. It was an unfamiliar feeling. Tenar still had not moved. How could she be sure? She had imagined things happening in such a different way. Which choice was right? And if she did not go . . . ? Would she ever find the Stranger? Anastasia felt the echo and weight of a thousand such moments.

"What do *you* want?" she finally asked. "What do *you* want more than anything?" It was the same question that Tenar had posed to her. The question she could not answer.

Tenar did not hesitate. "God," was the reply. "In whatever way God comes. In every form, through every experience and circumstance, painful or otherwise. God. Only God." The Magician's voice was soft, but the words filled the space between them, and their meaning blazed with love.

Sunlight fell across Anastasia's face, and she raised a hand to shield her eyes. A small bird flew to her feet. Instinctively she understood that she knew as much as she could know at that moment. She had to make a choice.

With all her heart she wanted to join the Magician, but that same heart was afraid. She was not sure she was ready to know the things she might learn if it also meant everything would change. The same fear that frightened the people of Status and Quo had followed her into the forest. She could see it holding her back, but she felt unable to move. Her fear of change felt greater than her longing.

After several uncomfortable minutes, Anastasia turned back toward her familiar clearing. She could feel the Magician standing behind her, watching as she started to walk away. She simply could not follow.

The next months made any earlier hardships seem small. Nothing satisfied her now. Nothing made sense. She questioned everything. Her search began to seem pointless and every anxiety intensified. She tried to keep all thoughts of Tenar from her mind, but the memory of their meeting was always there. Maybe what she wanted, more than anything, was to hold on to the things that made her life feel secure. Maybe she wanted assurance that she would never have to change or be uncomfortable. But she had those assurances now, and they brought no peace.

It was the most difficult Winter of her journey. She twisted her ankle jumping from a ledge and hobbled on a homemade crutch for weeks. The snows were deep, the winds biting.

When Spring arrived she was beginning to see herself as she really was: frightened . . . and just as devoted to sameness and security as those she had once criticized. She was apparently afraid to know and speak her own voice. She had asked relentless, challenging questions in Status and Quo. But when she was offered an opportunity to create a new possibility for her life, she had chosen to cling to old ways and cherished ideas. The hardest thing to face was a nagging feeling that something true had stood before her, and she had walked away.

As buds began to appear on ripening branches, Anastasia began to let herself hope that the Magician would also mysteriously reappear. She had thought deeply throughout the Winter and greatly regretted not going with Tenar.

Didn't she already know where fear and caution led? What she *didn't* know was where courage and love could take her. Her heart called out as she walked, longing for a second chance, a chance to choose differently. Several nights she found herself praying like a child for Tenar's return. And as she climbed through the Mountain passes, her eyes searched every grove of trees for a sign.

Eventually, Summer passed into Fall, and the leaves turned brown and began to drop. Anastasia continued making her way across streams and high mountain ridges. Early one morning as she bent to touch a flower growing in the cleft of a rock, a sudden shading on the rock caught her eye. She sat back on her heels as a shadow fell across her face.

"I can't believe you came back!" she managed to say.

"You called from your heart, " replied Tenar.

This time there was no magic pool and no conversation. No questions, no answers. Anastasia sensed that a second chance is not lightly given.

There was still no certainty to hold onto. The Magician's eyes and face were still inscrutable as Anastasia searched them for clues or reassurances. Her choice would have to be her own. What did she want? She knew herself well enough now to know she couldn't give a perfect answer.

She saw all that she did not know, and how much there was to understand.

Tenar watched her for a while and then turned, walking toward the next summit.

Fear still reached out to her. It had not gone away. But this time she chose to follow the Magician. Fear would have to make this journey with her. Stooping to bid good-bye to the flower, she jumped to her feet and ran down the path where Tenar was walking.

Hearing her footsteps, the Magician turned back to wait.

"I have seen too many stars

to let the darkness overwhelm me."

—*Macrina Wiederkehr*

Part Three
Anastasia

Paula D'Arcy

*A*nastasia and the Magician did their most rigorous climbing in the earliest part of the day. They arose before dawn, when Anastasia's hands were still cold from the morning chill. Tenar usually walked ahead, clearing a path. Anastasia walked more slowly, searching for the first signs of the sun. When the first light appeared above the distant peaks, its fire rested on her face. As they walked she listened, eagerly awaiting each turn, never knowing what they might encounter on the path ahead. In this way their journey settled into an expectant rhythm.

Without understanding why, Anastasia often felt a strange stirring when she was with her teacher, as if a tiny flame deep within her responded to the look in Tenar's eyes. At times the Magician's look could be far away, and yet, at the same moment, Tenar was completely present.

Anastasia was filled with questions. "Why are you a magician? What kind of magic do you perform? Where did you learn the things you know? Where have you come from and why are you here, in these Mountains? When did the Stranger enter *your* life?"

And even though she knew Tenar was fond of her, still, her queries were rarely answered. The usual response to her curiosity was silence.

Eventually this moved Anastasia to reconsider her questions . . . and her reasons for asking them. Often, when she thought further about why she had posed a particular question, she would withdraw it. Sometimes, in the quiet, she found her own answer. And she grew to understand that what mattered to Tenar were not her words or her inquisitiveness, but her readiness to pay attention to everything around her. And after a while, she began to listen.

In time she realized that if she walked alongside Tenar as a child would, looking in wonder at all that surrounded her, she could find delight in the smallest things. But if she got lost in her thoughts, trying to analyze and make sense of things, she found the day tedious and long. 'How amazing,' it occurred to her, 'that I should need the help of this Magician to see what I once saw so easily as a child.'

✝

"Did you enjoy learning when you were in school?" Anastasia asked Tenar one morning. They had been picking blueberries the bears had not discovered and were sitting in a shady spot, enjoying their cache. Her question was prompted by her concern that she had learned so little of all there was to know.

Tenar looked at her thoughtfully. "A person must have knowledge. The world demands it. But when we try to use words to describe the greatest things, they become smaller. When we try to explain our inner Knowing with language, it loses meaning. It changes. That is why silence can sometimes tell us so much more."

Tenar smiled and looked around. "That is also why I love to be in these Mountains. Here, things do not need an explanation. Here, inner Knowing is in harmony with everything around it."

"So will you stay in the Mountains forever?"

"No, Little Friend." The Magician grinned and tugged at her sleeve. "Anyone can find what is beautiful and true by living apart from ordinary life. Everyone is enlightened on the mountain top. The harder choice is to live with the Knowing right in the center of your life. In your daily chores. In the middle of a family. In places of commerce. The challenge is to find what is beautiful and true in ordinary life."

Anastasia continued to be fascinated by the Magician. Tenar was unlike anyone she had ever known. It was impossible to remain ignorant of foolish acts or mistaken ideas in the presence of her teacher. Whenever her fears and fantasies got in her way, she quickly became aware of them in her guide's presence. Tenar seemed to be a light that helped her see clearly.

But sometimes she found herself looking at things it would have been easier not to see. Was this the magic? The Magician had never referred to it by any name. The chance to *see* was simply there, if she really wanted to grow.

"Tenar, what is God like?" Anastasia suddenly asked the Magician one day, hoping to receive an answer she could understand.

Leaning forward to smell the fragrance of a nearby branch of rosemary, the Magician remained silent for a few moments.

"God is not an idea or a concept for you to grasp," her teacher finally replied. "God is not something to be studied or something to define. No definition would be wide enough." Tenar paused and looked directly into Anastasia's eyes. "God can never be fully contained by words or be understood by the human mind."

"Then . . . ?"

"You cannot define God, Anastasia, but you can be *with* God. You can *know* God."

She hated to ask, but she wanted to understand. "How?"

"Look around you and pick something up," said Tenar. "Choose something that is not perfect."

Anastasia looked around quizzically. Stones? No. How were they imperfect? A leaf? A flower? Even a weed? Wasn't everything what it was meant to be? But Tenar would say no more.

+

Later that day, when it was too hot to move, they sat on a flat, reddish stone at the base of a small creek. In front of them, growing from the rock, were magnificent purple flowers. Two of the flowers were buds, the third, fully blossomed. Anastasia lay down on her side, watching. "Soon the two buds will be as beautiful as the blossom that has already opened," she murmured.

Tenar did not respond, but Anastasia sensed the Magician had something to say. More and more she was able to be patient, listening to the language of silence. As she continued to watch the flower and listen to the tumbling waters of the creek, she decided to tuck the moment away and ask about it later. She did not want to interfere with the stillness.

All that day, they sat on the same rock without a spoken word. When they finally moved on, Anastasia felt a great sense of fullness in her heart.

✝

Sometimes the Magician would leave Anastasia alone, saying, "I will be back in a little while." The first time it happened Anastasia was frantic, convinced she had done something wrong. Had she been too noisy? Too curious? Too quiet? Not bright enough? Disappointing? Probably it was taking her too long to learn. Was Tenar reconsidering being her teacher? Would the Magician return?

All these questions made it difficult to think clearly. It took her a while to realize that Tenar had left purposefully. It was only when she was alone in the forest that she could see how much fear still colored her thinking. In the stillness of dawn, she could hear her own inner arguments. In the cold night air, she could feel how much she held on to comforting, familiar beliefs.

And it was only in the quiet that she could truly listen to the language of silence. When she was still, she could hear Nature's voice. It encouraged her not to be afraid, to trust the Mystery that unites all things.

When the Magician did come back, they continued as they had before. One afternoon they were searching for small kindling to build a fire.

"I learn more and more about myself every day," Anastasia remarked. "I continue to see how much I don't know, and how ignorant I am of many things. Is this the hardest part, realizing how much I will never understand?"

Reaching for a fallen cedar bough that had rolled into a thicket, Tenar did not look up from the ground. "No, Anastasia, recognizing how much you don't know is not the hardest thing."

She was thoughtful for a moment. "Oh, then I know. The hardest step must be just the opposite: To find out all that I am capable of understanding!"

Smiling gently, Tenar walked toward her, holding out the bough. "Ah, Little One, you try so hard. But there is another choice."

Anastasia sat on the ground in frustration. How could you know things you had not worked hard to understand?

"The hardest step, Anastasia, is to *be*. Not to think. Not to understand. Just to *be*. This is the most difficult thing. Nature does it easily. It can be what it is. It has no other intention. A tree does not wish to be an animal. A flower does not wish to be a vegetable. Nature accepts how things unfold. And She teaches you these secrets if you listen."

Anastasia moved to add the bough to the fire. The sparks crackled as she laid it on the coals.

"Do you remember how the Stranger taught that each Human Being is unique? Sometimes, however, people wish to be many things they are not, and they forget they are created in the Great Spirit's image and are connected to a greater Love. They forget they are who God created them to be. Like the elders of your town, some people insist on certain beliefs and ideas, and they work very hard to make sure that everyone has the right facts. What they have forgotten how to do is to be *with* God."

"How can I do that?" Anastasia interrupted, wrinkling her brow as she struggled to understand.

"By remembering that you can never be separated from the Being who gave you life. You were created by the Love that gives life to all things. Human love is a way to touch *this* greater Love. That is its purpose."

"Is that what happened when I fell in love with Peter?"

"Yes and no. Sometimes when people experience 'being in love,' they briefly get a hint of something greater. When your heart opened to Peter, for a short while you saw things more clearly. You felt expansive.

"When love occurs," continued the Magician, "it appears to be something happening only between two people. But thinking of it in that way makes love very small and ordinary. When you *truly* love, it is the beautiful Being you are seeing and loving, even though your eyes may be looking at another person. If you let love lead you, it will carry you to the greater Love. And your eyes will be opened to many beautiful things."

"If love is so beautiful," Anastasia responded slowly, looking into Tenar's eyes and choosing her words with care, "then why do we not choose Love all the time? Why are we content to see in a smaller way?"

The Magician watched the fire. "Love is very powerful, Anastasia. Love makes unexpected things happen. Love changes everything. And change makes many people uncomfortable. Some would prefer to feel safe. People also do not choose love because they are not yet ready. It is not their time."

"Some people are ahead of others?"

"Not in terms of being 'better than.' Only in terms of readiness." Tenar was thoughtful for a moment. "Anastasia, do you remember the purple flowers we saw several days ago, growing from the rock?"

Anastasia nodded.

"The blossom was not more beautiful than the buds. All the stages of the flower are equal in their beauty. The seed. The first green shoot. The bud. The blossom. None is greater or higher in value. They are all stages of readiness. And truly, they all exist already. The blossom already exists in the seed. Everything already is.

"It is the same with people. The awakening that will one day occur is already there now. And when people are ready, they will have full sight and know what is true. No one owns this process. Only the Great Being holds the truths waiting to be known.

"Who has greater knowledge, or who is 'ahead' of someone else in their awakening is not important. Some flowers bloom earlier, but they are not better flowers."

"Just one more question?"

"Yes, Anastasia, *one* more question!" Tenar's great eyes were filled with mirth.

"Is there nothing I can do to help myself become more ready? Can anything move me along?"

Tenar spoke so softly she had to lean forward. "Desire, Anastasia. If you have a true desire to be closer to God. God cannot resist love."

✝

"We have been journeying together for such a long while." Anastasia was picking blackberries, filling a small wooden bowl Tenar had carved from a fallen limb. "When we began, I thought you would take me directly to the Stranger. Each time we climbed a new mountain, I expected to see him there."

"Are you disappointed?"

"No. I know you will bring me to him when the time is

right. In the meantime, I'm so content to be with you. I do not know how to say thank you. There is so much to learn."

Even as she spoke, her eyes filled with tears. "Sometimes I ask myself if God is really within me, or if I exist within God."

"Sit beside me, Anastasia." Tenar patted the hollow of a fallen white oak. "The only way to be with God is through love. Love is always the way. Always."

"Oh, Tenar, I grow so impatient. Last night I had a dream. I was looking through the window of a large house, deep in the forest. Someone who had been guiding me came to the door. I heard the being call me to come, but I could not see the being with my physical eyes. When I went outside, I was blinded by the light. Then something began to guide me from within, and suddenly there was a child in front of me who could see. I began following her. We were almost dancing as we walked. I was aware of an immense, loving power.

"Tenar, I once believed I was in pursuit of this power. In the dream I could see that the Loving power was pursuing me. It was everywhere. It consumed the universe, and I wanted to live in that Love. All I wanted was to be with it."

✝

They had been climbing steadily for many days. Just when the summit seemed near, another peak appeared. When they started out, the only sign of water had been the small creek running over pebbles. But with each step of ascent, the water had become more noticeable in its power. They followed its sound, crisscrossing the stream beds until waterfalls began to appear. Gentle at first, the cascades became more thunderous. By mid-afternoon they had to sit shoulder to shoulder in order to speak over the roar. They were finally at the water's deepest source.

Tenar leaned closer toward Anastasia's ear. "Spirit expresses Herself in countless ways. She is power. She is knowledge. Everything is Hers. She allows herself to move inside matter and form. Everything that comes from her womb is an expression of Love. Look around you. Nothing exists without Her willing it. Nothing is separate from Her love. Nothing."

"Does that mean everything is holy?" asked Anastasia.

"Everything is holy because of this Love. Only Love." Tenar's voice was a whisper. "We live in this love without even suspecting it."

At the end of the day, they camped at a spot where the roar of water could still be heard, its song a source of endless music. Listening well into the night, Anastasia remembered her first meeting with the Magician, when she had tried to decide what she *really* wanted.

'Use your inner Knowing,' Tenar had advised. 'It will show you the way. Peel back all the layers until you know that which exists deep within your heart. That is where your soul dwells, a living form of the Great Soul. A true spark from the fires of heaven.'

That night she watched while Tenar slept. As the hours passed, she sat without moving, drawn to the beauty in all the images that came and faded with the changing moon. By morning light, she still sat quietly, aware of the mist in the air and the fading stars. Reflections of each of these fell over Tenar, and she watched with love.

Then her eye caught sight of an open notebook, and she saw these words, written in the Magician's hand:

"Read this, Anastasia."

She picked up the pages carefully and began to read:

> *A Stranger came to a distant land*
> *one summer day, long ago.*
> *He was guided there the same way*
> *seeds are taken by the wind*
> *to places unknown.*

> *The Stranger spoke the truths*
> *that time had stamped in his soul*
> *by the fire that burns*
> *in the heart of all things.*

The Stranger met with the children
beside the river,
and they danced and flew kites.
And the Stranger spoke words
from his heart to theirs.

And a fire was lit
in the secret chambers of the souls
of those who came to listen.

The Stranger told them
about a Beautiful Being
whose only desire was love.

"Listen for the Knowing," he said,
"that the Great Being
placed inside of you.
It will remind you who you truly are.
Remember that you cannot be separated
from the Being who gave you life."

And as the days went swiftly by,
one particular child listened more and more,
until one day her soul,
awakened by the sound of the Stranger's voice
and the love in her heart,
rushed to the surface
and called out her name.

Anastasia.
One who will be born anew.
O great wonder!

In time the Stranger met her again,
leading her deep into the forest,
across valleys and into the Mountains.
The Stranger climbed with her,
teaching her to know the trees,
the flowers, the clouds.

"What do you truly want?"
the Stranger had asked her.

She looked at her world
through the eyes of her heart.
She learned to listen to the language of silence,
and new sounds invaded the chambers of her soul,
crashing like a mighty waterfall.

She sought the Spirit,
and Love responded.

And in that moment, as Anastasia finished reading the
Magician's words, she searched the face of Tenar who
still lay asleep by the smoldering fire. Although she had
looked into this familiar face many times, she now recognized what she had not seen before. A deeper Knowing stirred within. The sun that fell on her face was no

longer incidental. She felt the power in the stillness at dawn and heard, finally, the voice of the water. She had found in her heart what she truly wanted. But there were no words to describe it. It simply was.

And it changed everything.

Paula D'Arcy

Past fears which Bind me

Potent Red Fire of New Sight

Changing all I am

—Anastasia

EPILOGUE

Many years passed before Anastasia returned to the towns of Status and Quo. She purposely arrived at night, reaching the river's edge in the darkness. She walked slowly along the bank, listening to the water. She was by herself, but not alone.

A crescent moon cast a slim shadow over the grasses. She remembered the Stranger's kite. She felt the children, dancing in a circle. She could picture the knapsack she had carried when she crept out of town. In the middle of the ordinariness of all the things around her, she saw the face of Tenar. Love surrounded her.

'I had no idea,' she thought. 'I simply had no idea.'

She sat by the river, letting her hand trail in the water, feeling its coolness. It was a small river running through two insignificant towns. Of themselves they had no particular meaning. The only meaning was the one her eyes brought.

She stood still, letting her eyes linger, watching the Fire.

PAULA D'ARCY lives in the Texas Hill Country, and her time is spent writing and leading retreats and conferences. She is the author of *Song for Sarah, When Your Friend Is Grieving,* and *Gift of the Red Bird*. As a therapist, Paula has ministered extensively to those facing grief and loss, drawing upon the personal loss of her own husband and child in 1975. She is also President of the Red Bird Foundation, which supports the growth and spiritual development of those in need throughout the world. Her grown daughter, Beth Starr D'Arcy, pursues a career as a professional actress.